Dear Parent:

Congratulations! Your child is taking the first steps on an exciting journey. The destination? Independent reading!

STEP INTO READING® will help your child get there. The program offers five steps to reading success. Each step includes fun stories and colorful art. There are also Step into Reading Sticker Books, Step into Reading Math Readers, Step into Reading Phonics Readers, Step into Reading Write-In Readers, and Step into Reading Phonics Boxed Sets—a complete literacy program with something to interest every child.

Learning to Read, Step by Step!

Ready to Read   Preschool–Kindergarten
• big type and easy words • rhyme and rhythm • picture clues
For children who know the alphabet and are eager to begin reading.

Reading with Help   Preschool–Grade 1
• basic vocabulary • short sentences • simple stories
For children who recognize familiar words and sound out new words with help.

Reading on Your Own   Grades 1–3
• engaging characters • easy-to-follow plots • popular topics
For children who are ready to read on their own.

Reading Paragraphs   Grades 2–3
• challenging vocabulary • short paragraphs • exciting stories
For newly independent readers who read simple sentences with confidence.

Ready for Chapters   Grades 2–4
• chapters • longer paragraphs • full-color art
For children who want to take the plunge into chapter books but still like colorful pictures.

STEP INTO READING® is designed to give every child a successful reading experience. The grade levels are only guides. Children can progress through the steps at their own speed, developing confidence in their reading, no matter what their grade.

Remember, a lifetime love of reading starts with a single step!

To George, a super nephew!
—J.E.B.

For Tom F. Deitz, a wordsmith and a visionary
—L.W.

For Sam
—D.T.

DC SUPER FRIENDS and all related titles, characters, and elements are trademarks of DC Comics. Copyright © 2010 DC Comics. All rights reserved. Published in the United States by Random House Children's Books, a division of Random House, Inc., 1745 Broadway, New York, NY 10019, and in Canada by Random House of Canada Limited, Toronto.

Step into Reading, Random House, and the Random House colophon are registered trademarks of Random House, Inc.

Visit us on the Web!
www.stepintoreading.com
www.randomhouse.com/kids

Educators and librarians, for a variety of teaching tools, visit us at
www.randomhouse.com/teachers

Library of Congress Cataloging-in-Publication Data
Bright, J. E.
Brain freeze! / by J. E. Bright.
        p. cm. — (Step into reading. Step 2)
"DC Super Friends."
Summary: Batman, Superman, Cyborg, the Flash, and the Green Lantern must battle Mr. Freeze when he encases Metropolis's central computer in ice and shuts down the city.
ISBN 978-0-375-86221-2 (trade) — ISBN 978-0-375-96221-9 (lib. bdg.)
[1. Superheroes—Fiction.]
I. Title.
PZ7.B76485Br 2010   [E]—dc22   2009024718

Printed in the United States of America   10   9   8   7   6

BRAIN FREEZE!

By J. E. Bright

Illustrated by Loston Wallace and David Tanguay

Random House 🏠 New York

It is a big day

in Metropolis.

A new computer will
control everything.

The computer
is called the Brain.
It will run the trains.

It will control
the traffic lights,
the water supply,
and the power.

Superman pulls
the switch that turns
on the Brain.

Mr. Freeze wants
to give Metropolis
brain freeze!

Mr. Freeze fires

his ice cannon.

The Brain is frozen solid!

The city's water
stops running.

The power goes off.

A train speeds out of control!

Superman and the Flash

zoom into action.

Superman stops

the train.

The Flash helps
the riders.

Cyborg tells the cars when to STOP.

Green Lantern tells
them when to GO.

Batman swings down on Mr. Freeze.

Batman's feet
get frozen.

Superman breaks the ice.

Mr. Freeze runs

to his ice cannon!

Superman uses
his heat vision
to melt the cannon.

"Get ready to cool off
in jail,"
Batman says.

Superman thaws

the Brain.

It still works!

Teamwork saves
the city.

The Super Friends celebrate with ice cream!